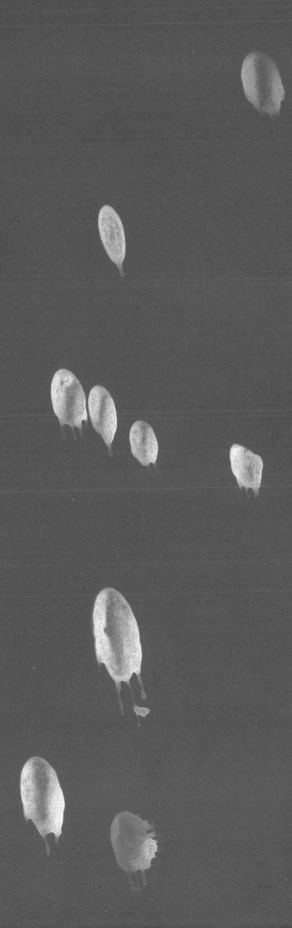

FEROCIOUS WILD BEASTS!

For Tristan, Rhys, and Stefan

THIS IS A BORZOI BOOK PUBLISHED BY ALFRED A. KNOPF

Copyright © 2009 by Chris Wormell

Published in the United States by Alfred A. Knopf, an imprint of Random House Children's Books, a division of Random House, Inc., New York. Originally published in 2009 in Great Britain by Jonathan Cape, an imprint of Random House Children's Books.

Knopf, Borzoi Books, and the colophon are registered trademarks of Random House, Inc.

Visit us on the Web! www.randomhouse.com/kids

Educators and librarians, for a variety of teaching tools, visit us at www.randomhouse.com/teachers

Library of Congress Cataloging-in-Publication Data
Wormell, Christopher.
Ferocious wild beasts! / Chris Wormell — 1st American ed.
p. cm.
Summary: When a boy wanders into the forest where he has been warned about the dangerous wild animals, he encounters nothing of the sort.
ISBN 978-0-375-86091-1 (trade) — ISBN 978-0-375-96091-8 (lib. bdg.)
[1. Animals—Fiction. 2. Humorous stories.] I. Title.
PZ7.W88773Fe 2009
[E]—dc22
2008036373

The illustrations in this book were created using watercolor.

MANUFACTURED IN MALAYSIA
10 9 8 7 6 5 4 3 2 1
First American Edition

FEROCIOUS WILD BEASTS!

Chris Wormell

ALFRED A. KNOPF
NEW YORK

A bear was strolling in the forest
one day . . .

when he met a small boy,
sitting on a tree stump,
looking rather sad.

"What's the matter?" asked the bear.

"I'm lost," sniffed the boy, "and I'm in terrible trouble."

"Dear me, why's that?" inquired the bear.

"Because my mom said I must never go into the forest," replied the boy, "but I did. And now I'm lost!"

"Don't worry!" said the bear with a laugh. "I'll soon show you the way out. The forest isn't so bad, you know."

"It is!" declared the boy. "My mom says the forest is full of *ferocious wild beasts*!"

"Really?" said the bear. "Is it? What are they like?"

"They're all hairy," replied the boy. "And they hide in the shadows and then they pounce on you and gobble you up!"

"Do they . . . er, do they gobble up bears too?" asked the bear nervously.

"Of course," replied the boy. "They gobble up everything!"

The bear peered fearfully into the shadows between the trees. "I think we'd better go," he said.

They had not gone far when they met an elephant having a snack.

"Would anyone like a banana?" asked the elephant.

"You'd better watch out, Elephant," advised the bear. "This young man tells me there are *ferocious wild beasts* on the loose!"

"Oh dear!" said the elephant, dropping his banana. "Are they *very* wild?"

"The wildest beasts ever!" said the boy. "They're SO big they could step on you and squish you just like that!"

"But, er . . . they couldn't squish an elephant, could they?" asked the elephant.

"Easily!" replied the boy.

"Oh crumbs!" gulped the elephant.
"You don't mind if I tag along with you, do you?"
And soon all three were creeping through the forest.

Before long they met a lion sunbathing on a rock.
"Sit down and enjoy the sun!" said the lion with a
flick of his tail.

"Not likely!" replied the bear. "Don't you know there are
ferocious wild beasts about?"

"Are there?" gulped the lion. "How ferocious?"

"The most ferocious type of all," declared the boy. "And they have sharp claws and big teeth and can bite your head off in a second!"

"Yikes!" yelped the lion. "But they couldn't do that to a lion, could they?"

"I think they like eating
lions the best," replied the boy.
"Oh, help!" whimpered the lion,
his mane standing on end.
"You wouldn't mind if I came
along with you, would you?"

So off they went, tiptoeing through the forest.
And soon they met a crocodile . . .

and a wolf . . .

and a python.

Now the sun was sinking.
"The nighttime is when the ferocious wild beasts come
out to hunt," said the boy.

Just then they heard a sound . . .
like the sound of a terrible beast
stomping through the undergrowth.

Then they saw a light flickering through the tree trunks
like a great glowing eye. . . .

And then they heard a wild roar echoing through the forest. . . .

And they all ran for their lives!

Well, except for the small boy, who was
the bravest. He crept forward and saw that
it wasn't a ferocious wild beast at all—
it was something *much* worse. . . .

"*There* you are," she sighed. "Didn't I tell
you *never* to go into the forest?
Didn't I tell you about all the
ferocious wild beasts?"

"But, Mom," Jack protested,
"I didn't see any ferocious wild beasts."